THE DARK ROOM

AN EROTIC ADVENTURE

VICTORIA RUSH

VOLUME 2

JADE'S EROTIC ADVENTURES - BOOK 2

COPYRIGHT

The Dark Room © 2018 Victoria Rush

Cover Design © 2018 PhotoMaras

All Rights Reserved

✿ Created with Vellum

FEEL THE RUSH:

Jade's Erotic Adventures – Book 1

When lonely divorcée Jade seeks to broaden her horizons, she's invited to a private dinner event which promises to stimulate all of her senses. Wearing nothing but masquerade masks, dinner guests receive special service under the table while their fellow diners look on...

The Dinner Party

Jade's Erotic Adventures - Book 3

Jade discovers a yoga club where members stretch and explore each other's bodies in the buff. She books an appointment, and during the first session meets a young redhead who tantalizes her with her flexibility and stunning body...

Naked Yoga

Jade's Erotic Adventures - Book 4

When Jade looks for an exciting new adventure, she discovers a nude cruise where naked couples enjoy unusual shipboard activities. She books a cabin and on the first day meets a stunning brunette who volunteers to show her around...

Nude Cruise

For the uninhibited...

1

————

IN THE SHADOWS

After my exhilarating experience at The Dinner Party, I was ready for more sexual exploration. The idea of being watched and watching other people releasing our inhibitions in a group setting was incredibly erotic. There was something about being with strangers that took the encounter to an entirely new level.

But it was more than that—it was the *anonymity* that made it especially appealing. With my mask on, I felt empowered to try new things, to do things I would never do in my regular guise. It was like I had superpowers. With my identity hidden, I could try anything, and the results were equally surprising. The sexual feelings were stronger and the climaxes were more powerful than anything I'd experienced before.

I wanted more. But I also wanted something different. I wanted to stretch my boundaries to see how far my new powers of sexual expression could take me. What other exotic destinations might I discover in the erotic underworld?

One day late at night, I sat down in front of my computer

and typed in the search words 'anonymous group sex'. Among a litany of listings for gay bathhouses, swingers parties, and wife-swapping groups, I found a cryptic heading on the bottom of the second page, reading *The Dark Room: Explore Your Sensuality*. I clicked on the link and a video opened with a naked dancer undulating under the mesmerizing effect of black and white zebra-like stripes illuminated on her body.

I watched, transfixed, as the light patterns flowed over every sensuous curve of her body. In the background, soft instrumental music added to the trance-like effect. The alternating dark and light patches provided just enough camouflage to mask her identity. But as the light parts moved over different areas of her physique, they briefly revealed her erogenous zones. The curve of her shapely breasts, a fleeting glimpse of her bare nipple, the glorious cleft in her tight round ass. She was completely naked, but I had to look carefully to recognize the naughty parts.

And what a sight it was to behold. As the illuminated stripes curved and stretched around every contour of her body, they accentuated her gorgeous figure. When she moved closer to the screen and briefly revealed her face, it had the same effect. I could see the fullness of her lips and the sensuous curve of her cheekbones. But the light never stayed in one place long enough to betray her identity, even if someone knew who was hidden behind the unusual light effects.

Now this was something completely different, I thought. Erotic, stimulating, and anonymous.

But where were her playmates?

As exciting as I imagined it might be to dance naked under the relative obscurity of these light effects, it would be infinitely *more* fun to participate actively with others in such a room. I scanned the webpage and noticed a heading in the menu at the top of the page titled 'Group Packages'. I clicked the link and three more video thumbnails appeared on the page: one labeled 'Men', one titled 'Women', and another marked 'Mixed'. I tapped on the first one, and another video started playing, showing multiple figures gyrating to the music.

This time, the light-projections were in different colors, shifting and bending around the moving figures like a psychedelic kaleidoscope. The bodies were masculine, with broad shoulders, muscled chests, and washboard stomachs. Occasionally, the men would brush up against one another and move their hips in a feigned anal intercourse motion, but the action was too slow and measured to be real. And the camera never strayed far below the subjects' bellybuttons, so it was impossible to tell if they were actually aroused. Even though they occasionally embraced in lip lock, it all seemed staged and dispassionate, like strippers putting on a show in a dance club.

I wasn't much interested in watching gay sex anyway, even with buff Chippendale characters such as these, so I clicked the next video thumbnail labeled 'Women'. This was definitely more my thing, and I could feel the stirring in my pussy as I reflected back on my last lesbian encounter at The Dinner Party. The video began with three slim and shapely women dancing sensuously under a new light effect. Instead of black and white alternating zebra stripes, this time the illuminated light resembled streaking raindrops.

The effect was even more captivating than the previous videos. Like an animated expressionist painting, the streaks danced across every curve and valley of the women's bodies as they swayed their hips and torsos in tantalizingly rhythmic ways. I had to concentrate even harder to catch fleeting glances of their breasts, nipples, and midsections, with the light patches even sparser than before.

At least in the women's videos, the camera panned below their waists to highlight the resplendent shape of their hips and buttocks. I strained to recognize the telltale protrusion of their mound or catch a glimpse of the mysterious slit between their legs. But as my pussy began to moisten imagining what was hidden behind the dancing raindrops splashing across their figures, the models never bent in such a way to reveal anything explicit.

Maybe this was the intention of the producers—to tease our interest just enough so we'd want to click for more information, leading to some kind of sale. This was, after all, the tried and true model for virtually every porn site—to show the viewer just enough to get them worked up until they were horny enough to pay for the real thing. Although in this case, I was still confused as to what the 'real thing' was this website was selling.

Was it just beautiful videos, orchestrated to appear as legitimate art? Were they just trying to sell me a fancy video version of a self-portrait that I could share with my husband or partner? That might be intriguing, but I was looking for more. As I continued watching the video, the three women moved closer to one another, eventually rubbing their hips and torsos together like in the all-male video. But this time, I could see their lower bodies as they caressed one another.

I watched them rub their hips and breasts together as the light streaks raced across their erect nipples. They were kissing one another far more sensuously than the men, like they were really losing themselves in the moment. It was definitely a turn-on and I imagined myself in the mix, caressing their beautiful bodies in the darkness with the streaks of light providing fleeting glimpses of their figures. As I thought about what it would feel like to have a stranger stroking my body in the dark, I slipped my fingers under my panties and began to play with my clit. But just as the action started flowing in the video, the clip suddenly ended.

Fuck! I screamed. *Just as I was getting turned on! Even a normal porno is better than this. At least they go all the way and offer some release.*

I was tempted to divert to my favorite porn site and watch some good lesbian tribbing action to get off when I noticed the last video thumbnail on the screen, labeled 'Mixed'. At least *this* one, if it was real, would be hard to hide the state of arousal that heterosexual men would experience in the presence of sexy naked women—light or no light.

I clicked on the icon, and the last video started to play. This time the light effects were in the form of multi-hued geometric circles, stretching and undulating over the curves of the naked figures like a rolling spirograph. I had to give it to the video producers—they were certainly creative in using unusual light effects that looked beautiful when projected onto shapely naked bodies.

And there was no denying that the bodies were gorgeous. Both the men and the women were firm and well-toned, with curves in all the right places. Every one of them was seriously fuckable. But much to my chagrin, the interaction between the subjects in the video once again seemed practiced and restrained. Even the men hardly seemed into it, rubbing and caressing their partners like in a cheesy black-and-white B-movie. The camera never strayed below their waistlines, but I didn't need to see their flaccid penises to recognize play acting when I saw it.

If this is what happens in these dark rooms, you can count me out, I thought.

It was all too antiseptic and 'soft-porn' for my liking. I wanted some *real* sex—actual *touching* and *penetration*—where I could feel myself and my dark room partners getting aroused and getting off. I didn't just want to be in some kind of frou-frou art production, I wanted to participate in a live orgy! I was about to click out of the website when a chat bubble popped up in the lower right corner. A text message appeared in the bubble.

'Hi!' someone named Sara wrote. 'How can I help you? Did you want to learn more about our products and services?'

Products and services? Maybe it's worth investigating this a little further after all. Let's see what other 'services' they have to offer...

2

────

EYES WIDE SHUT

'How can I participate in these dark rooms?' I typed in the chat window.

'If you come to our studio,' Sara replied, 'you can join any room of your choosing at any time.'

Studio? This was sounding more and more like some kind of photography service to me.

'How many people will be in the rooms with me?' I typed.

'That depends what time of the day and week you come. Friday and Saturday nights are busiest, but we also schedule sessions during the day, between 2:00 and 4:00 p.m. You can book a session by clicking on the tab for Appointments at the top of the page. We normally only have two or three people in the afternoon rooms and up to ten maximum on Friday and Saturday nights.'

The word *sessions* was beginning to sound more intriguing to me. I decided to probe for more information.

'What kind of clothing should I wear in these sessions?' I asked.

'You can wear anything that makes you feel comfortable,

but most of our patrons choose to wear a minimum of accoutrements.'

'Including nothing at all?'

'Yes—if that's what makes you feel most comfortable.'

I loved how Sara kept dancing around the obvious question.

'How do the people in these dark room sessions typically *interact*?' I typed.

'That depends on what you're looking for and the kind of people that join you in the room.'

I hesitated for a moment before typing my reply.

'Is *touching* permitted?'

'Absolutely. That's what makes the experience particularly enjoyable. You're encouraged to explore each other's bodies in the privacy and safety of the dark room. Subject to the consent of each partner, of course.'

Now we're talking, I thought. Exploring each other's bodies was exactly what I was looking for. But I still had lots of questions pertaining to the privacy and safety parts.

'What if I don't want somebody to touch my body? How can I ensure my personal space will be respected?'

'We have a simple rule for everybody entering any of our dark rooms. All you have to do is brush someone's body away if you don't wish to be touched. Everyone is issued a safety bracelet before entering each room. If you feel threatened or forced to do anything against your will, all you have to do is press the alert button and an audio intercom will be activated. Any violators will be immediately removed from the room. You can ask for help at any time, but we rarely receive complaints from any of our patrons.'

I paused to let Sara's comments sink in. I liked the safeguards they had set up, but I didn't like the sound of audio recordings or being leered at by a bunch of security guards.

'What kind of privacy will I have? Will any audio or video recordings be made while I'm in any of the rooms?'

'Never,' Sara said. 'What goes on in the security of the dark rooms is between you and your consenting partners.'

I liked the sound of that.

'What about the video clips on your website?' I asked. 'Those were obviously recorded. Were those actual participants?'

'Those were paid actors, using our own models. I assure you, you will never be recorded while in one of our dark rooms.'

'What about your security personnel or anyone outside the room? Can they see what's happening inside?'

'Each dark room is enclosed in one-way glass all around,' Sara replied. 'You can't see out, but outside observers can see in. This allows patrons to observe the action in the room before committing to go inside. We find this adds to the excitement level for both those watching and those being watched. But the light effects in the room are always moderated in such a way to ensure your identity will be masked. The only thing outside observers can see, including our security staff, are the silhouettes of the people inside.'

Oh my god, I thought. *That sounds so hot.*

The idea of being watched, both within the room and from outside the room, while I got down and dirty with my dark room partners sounded incredibly stimulating. I suddenly became aware of how soaked my panties had become as I continued the dialog with Sara.

'What about...*hygiene*?' I asked tentatively. 'What protections do I have against the spread of diseases?'

Sara and I finally seemed to be talking about the same thing. I decided to dispense with any further niceties and cut right to the chase.

'Every dark room participant must provide a recent blood test from an accredited medical lab,' she replied. 'You must report negative for all known sexual or communicable diseases. You'll also need to submit to a brief exam with our accredited medical doctor on staff to ensure you do not have any open sores or infections that could be spread by physical contact. This is for the safety of all participants.'

Holy shit, these guys don't fool around. A gynecological exam is never fun, but if it's performed by a real doctor and it's not too intrusive, it's better to be safe than sorry.

'Will the exam be performed by a gynecologist? Is the doctor male or female? May I ask for his or her credentials before I submit to the examination?'

'It will be with a female gynecologist for female examinations and a male urologist for male examinations. Their credentials will be on display in the examining office, which is also maintained with the utmost hygienic cleanliness. The examination is external only and very brief.'

Okay, I thought. *Now that we know exactly what we're talking about here, let's get down to brass tacks.*

'What are your fees? And is this...you know, *legitimate*? I mean, it sounds like I'm paying for sex.'

Sara paused for a moment before replying.

'This is a private club in a private residence. Whatever consenting adults choose to do with each other on private property is entirely legal. There is a modest subscription fee to join the club. You can see our fees under the tab marked Rates.'

It was all starting to come together. Just like The Dinner Party erotic club I attended a few weeks ago, they had similar terms of service. In fact, their professionalism and attention to detail made me wonder if it might be run by the same operators. I just had a few remaining questions.

'Are there separate rooms for men and women?' I asked. I was definitely ready for some more girl-on-girl action, but I wasn't ready to rule out a little hetero fun too if the mood struck me.

'We have separate rooms for men-only, women-only, and mixed gender. You may enter the single-gender room that matches your sex and also the mixed gender room, if you so wish, during your visit.'

I was definitely getting more interested by the moment and based on how fast the wet patch between my legs was spreading in my tight jeans, so was my aching pussy.

I wondered if there'd be any equipment to recline onto if things got hot and heavy enough.

'Are there places to relax in each of the rooms, or are they standing room only?' I typed.

'There is small upholstered furniture in each of the rooms, as well as Liberator sex cushions to adjust your position. Everything has neon piping around the edges to help you find it in the dark, and the coverings are laundered after each session to ensure cleanliness. Your safety and comfort is our universal goal.'

Wow, I thought. *These guys have thought of everything.*

This obviously wasn't going to be some kind of seedy swingers' party where just anybody could walk in and fuck anything that moves. This sounded like a first-class operation that was sure to titillate and satisfy all my senses.

I paused as I considered any other questions or concerns that I might have before venturing out to their club.

'How long can I remain in each room?' I said. 'And when I wish to leave, where can I go to freshen up and get dressed?'

'We have separate change rooms and showers for both men and women. Strobe lights are used in these and other public rooms of the residence to protect your identity at all times. From the moment you enter any of our dark rooms to the moment you leave the building, no one will be able to identify you. The only person who'll ask for ID is the doctor who examines you. He or she will verify your blood report belongs to you and the physician is sworn by doctor-patient privilege to maintain your privacy.'

I unconsciously exhaled a long deep breath as I began to relax. All my concerns had been addressed and all my expectations were satisfied. This was the perfect outlet I was looking for.

'Thank you for being patient with all my questions,' I typed. 'I'll check your rates and schedules and book a session in the near future.'

'It's been my pleasure,' Sara said. 'I hope our club satisfies all of your desires. Feel free to chat again if you have any more questions. See you soon!'

Satisfy my desires, indeed. I had no doubt that it would. But right now, I needed some satisfaction that no one else could give me.

I tore off my leggings and threw them on the floor as I reached into my nightstand for my favorite rabbit vibrator. Then I turned the rotating beads and rabbit ears on maximum and plunged the dildo into my aching pussy, moaning in delight as I imagined the pleasures that awaited me in the mysterious dark room.

3

FOREPLAY

As I thrust the vibrator deep inside my snatch, I watched the all-girl dark room video on continuous loop. I was absolutely hypnotized by the swirling light effects rolling over their luscious bodies. Whenever the streaks illuminated their bare nipples and mounds, it made the effect all the more electrifying. My pussy made sexy slurping sounds as my juices sopped up the slick dildo sliding in and out of my hole.

I moaned like a dog in heat thinking about what it would be like to watch and touch these women in a *real* dark room. This experience would take my Dinner Party adventure to a whole new level. Instead of just sitting and watching passively while other people did things to me, in these spaces I could participate actively with whomever I pleased. My mind raced with all the things I wanted to do with these women—and maybe even some of the men in the mixed room. I wanted to fuck and be fucked by these mysterious apparitions.

When the women in the video started touching one another and rubbing their nipples together, I lifted my hips off the bed and thrust the vibrator deeper inside me. I angled the shaft so the oscillating tip massaged my G-spot, while I pushed the fluttering rabbit ears hard against my swollen nub. I could feel my orgasm building and I opened my mouth to kiss one of the models in the video as she did the same. When the tide finally swept over me, I clamped down hard over the pulsing vibrator and spasmed a long stream of powerful contractions.

I hadn't cum this hard since Jasmin had jilled me under the dinner table at the Dinner Party retreat. As I lay on the bed rolling my hips in post-orgasmic bliss, I closed my eyes and imagined myself dancing with the geometric light effects projected on my body. For a thirty-six-year-old, I still had a pretty damn fine figure with a tight ass, perky breasts, and a yoga-toned stomach. I wouldn't be the only one in the dark room admiring the physiques of my fellow participants.

I pulled the vibrator out of my pussy and stood up to admire myself in my full-length dressing mirror. I began to sway my hips and caress my breasts like the women in the video. I looked pretty good, but something was missing. I turned off the bedroom light and closed the drapes, then opened the bathroom door just enough to emit a thin sliver of light. I moved back from the mirror until the ray of light projected a narrow beam on my body.

It wasn't nearly as fancy as the light effects shown in the dark room videos, but it was enough to make me imagine I was there. I experimented with different positions as I watched the light illuminate different parts of my body in the darkness of my bedroom. Just as in the videos, it was fascinating to see how I could briefly reveal the naughty parts by moving in and out of the light. It was almost as exciting to watch my own body as it was the models in the video, and I began to caress my curves like a stripper in a dance club.

I'll have to work on my technique, I thought, analyzing my moves.

I had to be as irresistible as the models in the video if I hoped to attract the attention of men and women with similarly toned bodies.

But that can wait for later.

Right now, the only thing I could think about was booking an appointment for a dark room session as soon as possible. My vibrator, as entertaining as it was, would be no match for the real thing. I sat down again in front of my computer and clicked on the tab marked Rates.

Let's see if I have to pay an arm and a leg to touch some of these arms and legs.

It wasn't as bad as I imagined. There was a one-time subscription fee of $300, plus another $200 for each session. *Seems reasonable,* I thought. The gyno exam alone would cost that much or more in a regular doctor's office. Two hundred bucks for two hours or more of safe, titillating sex with multiple partners seemed like a bargain.

"Sign me up!" I thought out loud, clicking the tab for Appointments.

A registration page opened where they asked me to create an account. I paused for a moment as I considered my next move. I could use an alias and a fake email account, but I knew they'd also want a credit card to pay for the subscription.

So much for nobody knowing my identity other than the doctor who'll examine me.

I looked further down the page and saw a disclaimer promising that my email and credit information wouldn't be shared with anyone else, and that I wouldn't be sent any marketing information other than the confirmation of my appointment.

What the fuck, I said to myself. *Anybody running an internet business these days knows the surest way to lose customers is to share someone's online details without consent. Besides, I reveal a lot more personal financial information when I pay bills and do my banking online—this is pretty minor in comparison.*

I filled in the required fields to complete my registration, then scanned the schedule for available sessions. All the Friday and Saturday nights on the booking calendar were grayed out for the next three weeks.

This place is popular, I thought. *I guess that's a good sign.*

I imagined that meant most sessions would be pretty full and that I'd have my pick of partners to choose to engage with. I remembered Sara saying the daytime sessions were not as busy as the night sessions, so I clicked on the first available weekday. A new window opened indicating that I was about to reserve an afternoon session for the indicated date, then it asked me to fill in the credit card information to complete the transaction. I filled in the required details then clicked the Submit button. After about ten seconds of processing time, a window popped up from my email account confirming the payment and appointment.

Well, that's it, I thought. *I'm committed now.*

I could feel the blood flowing back into my pussy as my mind already started going where I'd been fantasizing for the last hour. I stood up and positioned myself again in the sliver of light emanating from the washroom.

Damn girl, I thought, admiring my figure as my fingers strayed down toward my warm cunny. *This is going to be fun...*

4

PEOPLE IN GLASS HOUSES

On my appointment day, I could barely contain my excitement. I drove out to the address provided in my email confirmation and was pleasantly surprised when I arrived at the destination. As with my previous experience at the dinner party, the facility was in a large country chateau. Just like the last place, I had to provide my registration username and password to be permitted access through the security gate. I drove up the long tree-lined driveway to an even larger mansion than before.

If this was any indication of the step up in the level of services that awaited me, I was all-in. I parked my car alongside five or six other cars in the guest parking section and walked over a cobblestone path up to the front door. I tapped on the large brass door knocker and was greeted a few seconds later by an attractive young woman in a smart business suit.

I guess there'll be no naked attendants in masquerade masks this time around, I frowned. *Maybe this place is run by a different operator, after all.*

Nevertheless, the interior appointments and finishings were on a par with the previous home, and I was eager to explore its special rooms.

"You must be Jade," the woman said, taking my coat and hanging it in the closet. "My name's Ali, and I'll be your host for the evening. Can I get you something to drink? Coffee, tea, a glass of wine?"

I was pretty charged up already and thought a bit of alcohol would help relax some of the inhibitions I was beginning to feel about getting naked with a group of strangers.

"I'd love a glass of white wine if you have it, thank you."

Ali motioned to an adjoining room with large French doors.

"Feel free to relax in our waiting room," she said, handing me a piece of paper and a pen. "If you can take a few moments to review and sign this waiver, this will help ensure our expectations are aligned. I'll be back in a few minutes."

I walked into a beautiful room with tall Palladian windows and sat down on the large leather sofa. I quickly reviewed the document, which was mostly concerned with the rules of engagement in the dark rooms. Only women were permitted in the women's dark room it said, and only men were permitted in the men's dark room, but they could commingle in the mixed room. It reiterated the 'golden rule' about touching others only with consent. A simple brush of the hand or step back from an advancing partner indicated that you did not wish to be touched. Any violators would be immediately removed from the room and banned from using the facility in future. I signed the document with my alias Jade and placed it face-up on the coffee table.

I noticed some picture books lying on the table with

familiar photos of naked people illuminated with similar light effects to the videos I'd watched earlier. I opened one of the books and flipped through the pages as I admired the beautiful figures of the models and the different light effects displayed in each image.

I hope the people in my dark room will be as pretty as these, I thought, feeling my panties start to dampen again.

A minute later, Ali returned with a large glass of wine, setting it down on the coffee table.

"I see you've been familiarizing yourself with our light productions," she said, noticing the open book laid out in front of me. "Did you have any questions before I take you to the viewing room?"

Viewing room? The voyeur in me liked the sound of that.

"So I'll have a chance to watch some of the dark rooms before I choose to enter one?" I asked.

"Of course," Ali said. "That's part of the fun. All of our dark rooms can be observed from the outside through one-way glass. You'll be able to watch the participants but they won't be able to see you. Most of our patrons find this to be a stimulating experience that helps put them in the mood. If you like what you see, you can then proceed to the doctor's office for a brief exam, after which you're welcome to enter your appointed rooms. Did you bring your lab test report with you?"

"Yes—of course," I said, fishing in my purse for the blood test.

Ali held up her hand to save me the trouble.

"Bring it with you and show it to the doctor when she examines you. Are you ready to head downstairs?"

"Absolutely," I said, pleased that just as Sara had promised earlier, no one had yet asked for anything that could reveal my identity.

"Allow me to escort you, then. Would you like to leave your wine glass here or bring it with you?"

"I think it's better that I leave it here. Something tells me that I'm going to need my hands free for other things."

Ali simply smiled and nodded. I followed her out of the sitting room and across a marbled foyer, where we paused at the top of a declining circular stairway.

"Our dark rooms are in the lower level, where we can control the light more effectively. There are three exits, including a direct exit to the guest parking area. You may leave at any time, or return to the main floor if you need further help."

Ali reached into one of her pockets and handed me a black wristband.

"This is your security bracelet. Please wear it at all times until you leave the building. If you feel uncomfortable at any time, all you have to do is press this button on the side of your bracelet and a security agent will come to your assistance immediately. But I think you'll find it will be quite unnecessary. Our patrons are very respectful of the stipulated rules. I believe you'll find the experience very safe and satisfying."

I nodded my head as I fastened the bracelet buckle behind my wrist.

Ali escorted me down the stairs and opened a door at the base of the steps. A white strobe light and soft instrumental music emanated through the open portal.

"It may take you a few moments to get comfortable with the flashing light, but this will protect your identity while you stay on the lower level. The light is sequenced in such a way to allow you to find your way around while also maintaining your anonymity. Each of the exits are clearly marked, as is the entrance to the doctor's office and the change rooms."

She motioned to three large glass cubes in the center of the cavern.

"Each of the dark rooms is marked according to gender. Which room would you like to see first?"

"Um..." I said, hesitating for only a moment. "I think I'd like to see the women-only room first."

Ali gently grasped my hand and escorted me to the first glass-enclosed cube. It was much larger than it appeared from the other side of the room, measuring roughly twenty feet square on each side and ten feet tall. Inside the floor-to-ceiling glass panels, I could see the familiar movement of furtive figures illuminated under the kaleidoscopic light. The rest of the room was pitch black so the only things illuminated by the projected light were the moving bodies.

I unconsciously moved closer to the glass, captivated by the swirling light effects and soft music. This wasn't some cheesy strip club with pounding music and bright lights illuminating a gaudy stage. The soft instrumental music combined with the pretty light effects projected a feeling of real class. My eyes widened as I watched the naked participants move around inside the room.

Just as in the video, they were swaying their bodies and caressing each other. But there was something different this time. Their hands and bodies were no longer touching each other with fleeting, artificial gestures. This time, they *lingered* and *probed* one another. Their action looked *purposeful*, not like the play acting in the video. Near the front of the glass, two women were locked in a tight embrace, passionately kissing and grinding their hips together in familiar motion. I could see their buttock muscles flexing as they rubbed their mounds together under the swirling light.

My eyes raced around the inside of the enclosure as I took it all in. In the far corner of the cube, I noticed some neon piping tracing the outline of a large sofa. I squinted my eyes to decipher a commingled figure twisting together as the geometric lights swept over a mass of tangled arms and legs. At first, it looked like a single person doing some kind of yoga movement, with her leg stretched over her shoulder. But as I looked more closely, I could see that the raised leg belonged to a woman lying on the sofa with her legs splayed apart. Another woman was resting on her knees, squatting between the prone woman's legs, rubbing their vulvas together, fucking her with rapid swings of her hips while she clasped the prone woman's elevated leg tightly against her breasts.

I gasped audibly and slumped over, unconsciously mimicking the movement of the woman on top.

"Shall I leave you now to enjoy the show?' Ali said, somewhere to my side.

I'd completely forgotten she was still there. I turned and saw her familiar outline flashing beside me under the white strobe light.

"Yes, I'll be fine now," I said, catching my breath and trying to sound composed.

"Wonderful," she said. "You're welcome to remain outside the rooms and watch as long as your session is booked, or enter your allotted rooms at your leisure. The entrance to the dark rooms is via the doctor's office, who'll validate your blood report and conduct a brief external exam before you move on. Remember that if you need help at any time, all you have to do is press the button on the side of your bracelet. I hope you enjoy your stay and that we'll see you again soon. Bye for now."

It was strange watching her talk as the white light flashed over her face. I could see her lips open and close in delayed jerky movements that didn't synchronize with her speech. It was a bit disconcerting and nothing like the flowing movement of the light projected inside the dark room, but it was sexy and mysterious in its own way. Just as she and Sara had promised, it was impossible to recognize her face through the intermittent flashes.

"Thank you, Ali," I said. "I'll let you know if I need anything."

I was glad to see her leave, because my pussy was pounding and my crotch was soaked from watching the action in the cube. As soon as she closed the door leading to the stairs behind her, I unclasped the top button of my jeans and thrust my hand under my panties. My fingers immediately found my opening and I inserted three fingers as far as they'd go inside me while I rubbed my palm against my aching clit. It couldn't have taken more than ten seconds for me to cum hard in my jeans as I watched the women scissoring on the couch in the dark room.

It was difficult to see the expressions on their faces under the shifting light, but I noticed the mouth of the woman on top widen as her movements became increasingly frenetic. Then she suddenly stopped and arched her back as she pulled her partner's elevated leg against her torso and spasmed her body in obvious climax. I longed to be there with them, feeling what they were feeling and listening to their moans of ecstasy as their love juices washed over one another.

After I came down from my orgasm, I suddenly became

aware that I wasn't the only one standing outside the cube watching what was going on inside. I noticed another figure standing about five feet to my side, and I glanced in her direction. The flashing light showed just enough to reveal a pretty woman with long hair and high cheekbones. Although I'd never recognize her in the plain light of day, her full lips and gently sloping jawline betrayed her beauty. I glanced down at her body and noticed the bulge of her full breasts in her blouse and the curvature of her hips and ass in her tight jeans.

I blushed in the dark thinking that she might have noticed me rubbing myself in the dark like some kind of creepy flasher. But she just peered at me and smiled.

"Pretty hot, huh?" she said, in a soft, sexy voice.

"Yeah," was all I could manage to pant.

"Are you going in?" she asked, matter-of-factly.

"Definitely," I said.

"Perhaps I'll see you in a few minutes then. I'm going to watch for a little longer to get my nerve up."

"Enjoy," I said, imagining her getting just as turned on as I did watching the action in the cube. Sara was right—it was almost as much fun *watching* the action as participating in it. But I was eager to feel the touch of another woman and experience the hypnotic light effects first-hand.

But those aren't the only body parts I'll be using, I thought as I headed toward the examining room.

5

———

INTO THE LIGHT

The gyno exam wasn't as bad as I anticipated, though it was pretty embarrassing walking into the examining room with a big wet patch in the crotch of my jeans. The doctor didn't bat an eyelash and simply asked me to disrobe and lie down on the examining table. The whole thing was over in a couple of minutes.

She examined me for any sign of open sores then reviewed my lab test and checked my driver's license to verify the report. Fortunately, I'd made a recent visit to my aesthetician to clean things up down below. My smooth pussy was bald and spotless, which made the examination all the faster and easier.

When she was done, she handed me a note with a number and a key code then directed me through a door leading into the women's change room. As with the other public sections of the lower level, a soft strobe light permeated the change room. In between the flashes, I could see a few women in various stages of undress going about their business in the locker room, but I paid them no attention. Part of me wanted to search for the pretty woman who I'd chatted with briefly outside the women's dark room, but I decided it was best to respect everyone's privacy. There'd be plenty of opportunity to engage more directly once I got inside the actual dark rooms.

I located a bank of lockers with combination locks and pulled out the slip of paper the doctor had handed me. I matched the number on the slip with the corresponding locker and entered the code on the tumblers to undo the lock. Inside the locker, there was a freshly-laundered terrycloth robe and towel. I removed my clothes and placed my belongings inside the locker, then put the robe on and carried the towel to one of the shower stalls. I could still feel the vestiges of dried-up lubrication coating my inner thighs, and I wanted to be as clean and fresh as I could be going in to the dark rooms.

As I turned on the shower and stepped under its gentle spray, I reflected back to the video with the rain drop effect. I imagined myself dancing in the dark room as the light streaks flowed over my body, turning and bending my figure to reveal every sensuous curve. I opened a fresh bar of soap and rubbed the silky pod across my breasts, under my arms, and between my legs. My body felt electrified, and for a moment I was tempted to rub another one out, but I decided to save myself for the real thing. I didn't want anything tempering the pleasure that awaited me. I finished the shower, then dried myself off and returned my towel to my locker. I hesitated for a moment, deciding whether to hang my robe in my locker too, or wear it out into the open spaces of the lower level.

Screw it, I said, placing it on the hook. *This whole experience is about letting myself go and losing myself in the moment. Besides, between the strobe lights outside the dark rooms and the light show inside the rooms, no one will be able to recognize me anyhow.*

I closed the locker and scrambled the tumblers, making a mental note of my locker number and combination code. Then I walked out of change room into the open space of the lower level and looked around. It felt liberating to be stark naked in the cool air of the basement under the pulsating strobe lights.

Each of the three dark rooms were bathed with different colored and patterned light effects. On each side of the cubes, illuminated gender symbols clearly indicated who was inside. The glass cubes looked from a distance like a holographic dance show, with three different 'theaters' to choose from. I walked toward the cube displaying two familiar circle-and-cross symbols, knowing the all-girl show was what had initially attracted me to the program.

When I got closer to the cube, I noticed the light patterns inside had changed from when I viewed it earlier. This time, the patterns were in the form of orange and black spots, making the figures inside the room look like human-shaped leopards. I could make out four distinct figures inside the enclosure. Two of the women were quite slim, with tight ballerina figures. The other two were more voluptuous, with full breasts and wide, curving hips. But they all looked mouth-watering gorgeous, bathed in pretty feline leopard spots.

I was transfixed watching the women circle one another like prowling cats in the dark. It didn't take long for the figures to blend together and begin rubbing against one another. I stood spellbound as they huddled their bodies together like a group of leopards feasting over prey.

I want to be their prey, I thought, swaying my body in synchronization with the women.

I looked around the enclosure and didn't see anyone else standing in the flashing light, so I decided it was time to join the action inside the room. A sign on one side of the cube read Open. I ran my hand over the glass near the sign and felt a handle, pulling the glass door toward me. For a moment, the outside strobe light intermixed with the flowing orange spots inside the room, and I was conscious of how chaotic it suddenly appeared. I immediately closed the door and the one-way glass blocked out the outside light, returning the room to its flowing orange and black leopard motif.

By now, the four women in the room had paired off and seemed preoccupied with their partners, so I stood to the side and swayed my hips to the music as I watched the hypnotic movement of their bodies. The women circled around one another as if stalking each other. It was exciting to watch them play-act to the theme of the light show. But the acting soon turned more serious as the couples moved closer together and began rubbing their bodies together. Soon, their lips locked together and I could see them kissing passionately as the light and dark spots flowed over their faces.

I was dying to get in on the action, but I didn't want to interrupt their connection. As I watched their hands slide down each other's bodies, my hands mimicked their movement. When their hips briefly separated and their hands moved between each other's legs, so did mine. I was the odd woman out, but somehow I didn't mind. I could feel the juices flowing down my thighs as my pussy watered in sympathy with the gyrating couples.

I began circling my button and was just about to push my fingers into my slit when suddenly the light in the room was interrupted once again by someone opening the door.

The shape of the body in the flashing light looked familiar, and I recognized the shoulder-length hair of the woman who'd stood beside me earlier. She closed the door, then paused for a moment as she looked around the room. Before long, she began walking in my direction then stopped about two feet in front of me. She smiled as the leopard spots flowed over her face and I suddenly felt weak at the knees once again.

Her body was even more beautiful in the buff than in her tight blouse and jeans. Her breasts were a full and firm, with a gentle ski-jump slope on the top. These were no fake balloon-shaped artificial tits—these were the real thing. I glanced further down and watched the leopard spots flowing over her hips as my mouth began to water. There was just enough light flowing over her pubic area to show that she was shaved bald like me. As she danced sensuously in front of me in the dark, her bare mound swayed slowly from side to side.

"My name's Emma," she said in a soft voice.

"Jade," was all I could reply, hypnotized by her beauty.

"Beautiful, isn't it?" she said, turning her face toward one of the couples locked in a passionate embrace.

"Stunning," I said, happy the music was playing softly enough to engage in quiet conversation.

"You look like quite a tasty feline yourself," Emma said.

"You too," I replied lamely.

Emma inched closer toward me, until we were about six inches apart. I could see her looking directly into my eyes as she smiled sexily at me.

"May I?" she asked.

I wasn't sure exactly what she had in mind, but whatever she wanted to do with me, I was game.

"Please," I panted.

She closed the remaining distance and I could feel her breasts push against mine as she locked lips with me. A jolt shot through my body as if I'd been lit on fire. I could feel the heat of her body and the perspiration on our chests as our breasts slid sensuously over one another. She slipped her tongue between my lips and I sucked on hers as we swirled our tongues together. Our hips met and we gently ground our mounds together. When she moaned in my mouth, I practically came from the passion of the moment.

There was something electrifying about being in the dark with a perfect stranger, our bodies pressed together, with these mysterious and beautiful light effects highlighting the curves and shadows of our bodies. I could feel my nipples hardening, and we separated for a moment as we tweaked them together, watching the orange spots highlighting our swollen tips.

I was hypnotized by the sights and sounds and I could feel the juices in my pussy building by the moment as they began to run down the inside of my thighs toward my knees. As if reading my thoughts, Emma's right hand began tracing a line down the side of my waist and curved over my hips toward my love box. I quivered as her hand got closer to my pussy. When she finally slipped her fingers into my cleft and traced them slowly up toward my clit, I gasped out loud.

"Yes," I exhaled onto her bare shoulder as I slumped my body against hers. I wanted her to plunge her fingers deep into me and bring me to a quick orgasm. There would be plenty of time to experiment with other things and for me to return the favor in a moment. Right now, I desperately needed to get off.

She inserted two fingers further inside me and stroked my G-spot, and our mouths joined together once again. Our tongues swirled and sucked one another while she caressed my insides. But her palm remained stubbornly fixed in place over my mound. I wanted her to move her hand over my aching clit, and I swiveled my hips in a vain attempt to create more friction. But Emma seemed to be holding back, savoring the moment, as if intentionally denying my pleasure.

"Let's move to the sofa," she said, taking her hand out of my pussy and weaving her fingers between mine as she led me to the neon-outlined rectangle at the far edge of the cube. I hardly even noticed the other women as we walked straight by them, my head was so swimming in anticipation of what Emma wanted to do with me on the sofa.

When we got to the neon lines marking the perimeter of the couch, she gently pushed me down onto its surface. When my buttocks rested on the cushion, she kneeled down beside me and kissed me hard on the lips while lowering me slowly onto the couch. Emma lay on her side beside me while she ran her left hand over my breasts and stomach, then she leaned in and sucked my erect nipples. It felt incredible and I hoped she'd soon move lower and administer the same kind of action on my aching clit.

But she seemed content with running her hands over me as she explored every curve and crevasse of my body. When her hand passed over my bare mound, I lifted one of my legs to permit freer access to my pulsating cunny. Instead, she swept her arm under my knee and pulled my other leg up until both legs were pointed straight up in the air. Then she stopped kissing me and lowered her face closer to my hips.

Finally! I thought. She's going to give me attention where I most needed it—in my aching pussy.

She positioned herself behind my exposed ass, then spread my legs apart until they formed a bent V-shape, with my thighs resting against my chest. My entire vulva was now exposed to her and I could feel my wetness trickling down my perineum toward my anus.

Now, Emma, I screamed inside. *Suck my aching twat,* I begged. *Take me into your mouth and lick my clit like you were playing with my tongue earlier. Slip your fingers inside me and fuck my twat like there's no tomorrow. Because right now, time is standing still and I'm not sure there's going to be another tomorrow.*

Emma paused, and I lifted my head to look in her direction. She looked up at me and smiled with a mischievous grin as the leopard spots flowed over her pretty face. Then she lifted herself up and positioned her hips over top of mine as she rested her thighs on top of mine and slowly lowered her vulva until it touched mine. The feeling when our pussies touched was indescribable.

We were both aflame in passion and soaked through and through between our legs. I could feel her labia interlacing with mine in a different kind of lip lock, and I threw my head back against the sofa cushion in utter ecstasy. I began rubbing my cunt furiously against hers, listening to the sound of our juices commingling as they slurped and sloshed in glorious union. It was dirty and raunchy and sexy, and something I'd been longing to try ever since my last lesbian encounter at the Dinner Party.

Just when I thought it couldn't get any more intense, Emma shifted forward a few inches and our clits suddenly touched.

"Fuck, yes!" I cried out loud as our eyes locked in the strange orange and while shifting lightness.

Her face looked exquisite as we began to grind our pussies together and she fucked me harder. I could feel the hardness of her clit as it flicked and over mine, and I moaned in blissful abandon. I felt the ache deep in my core beginning to build, but I wasn't ready to cum yet. I wanted to savor this moment and play with Emma on the precipice of pleasure as long as I could make it last.

Emma leaned forward and began to kiss me passionately as she began fucking my gaping hole more vigorously. We both moaned into each other's mouths as we savored the union of our most private parts in the soft orange light. Suddenly, Emma lifted her face above mine and moaned an otherworldly sound. I felt a gush of liquid spraying against my open pussy, filling me with her juices. Emma was squirting her wetness against me while she came hard between my legs. Any chance of holding back my orgasm any longer quickly evaporated as I fell over the cliff, spasming a long serious of hard contractions against Emma's sex. While our bodies jerked and spasmed at the height of pleasure, we watched each other gasp and moan in the swirling lightscape.

When our climactic contractions finally subsided, Emma collapsed onto my body and kissed me softly on my lips. For the longest time, we simply lay on our sides with our legs intertwined, kissing and giggling like two little girls.

"That was incredible," Emma whispered in my ear.

"We're not done yet," I said, smiling into her eyes. "This cat still has a lot more fight left in her."

OVER THE RAINBOW

Emma and I played for another hour or so in the women's dark room, experimenting with different positions and techniques, and we both came many more times. I was tempted to engage with some of the other women in the room, but I wanted to save myself for something else. I exchanged email addresses with Emma and we promised to stay in touch, then I exited the cube.

When I stepped back into the flashing light of the lower level, I glanced over at the men's room. There was something intriguing about watching men have sex with one another, and I was drawn to their shapes moving under a different kind of light effect. As I got closer to the enclosure, I noticed the light looked like little white tadpoles, swimming over the men's bodies while they moved about the room. Just as in all the other rooms, it was beautiful and hypnotic to watch.

Three men were facing each other near the front of the glass, grinding their hips together in a triangle formation. As they swayed their bodies, I could see they all had erections and were rubbing their cocks together in a coordinated frotting action. It was fun watching them slap their swords together like they were Three Musketeers in a playful fight.

Suddenly, the man nearest the glass knelt down and began licking the other two men's penises. It was incredibly erotic to watch him caress their hard-ons with his tongue and lips. It was hard to tell exactly how worked up the men on the receiving end of his ministrations were, but the little white tadpoles racing across their stomachs simulated the effect of sperm shooting out of their cocks.

Then the kneeling man moved up to the heads of their cocks and took both penises into his mouth. I'd heard of double penetration before, but this was an entirely different version from what I'd never seen. As the two men humped their hips slowly together, fucking the kneeling man's mouth, they began to kiss passionately. I was surprised how turned on I was getting watching the action, and I was soon ready to experience some dick of my own in the mixed room. As much as I enjoyed making love to Emma, some-times all I wanted was a hard, throbbing cock pounding my pussy to its limits.

As I turned toward the cube housing the mixed-gender participants, my kitty beginning to tingle even more strongly. This time, the light effects stretched and curved around the figures in beautiful rainbow-colored stripes. I recognized three figures in the cube: one woman and two men. I stood entranced watching the colored stripes stretch and bend around their curves as they danced and rubbed their bodies together, much like the three men were doing in the men-only cube. But this time, the woman was sand-wiched between the men as they bucked their hips against her from opposite sides.

I had to look closely to see their erections under the

bands of light, but they were quite noticeable—and *large*. The man facing the woman's front side has his cock pressed up against her belly, while she stroked it sensuously with one of her hands. The man behind her had his tool between her legs and every time he swung his hips forward, I could see its head poke in and out under her mound. With her other hand, she caressed the underside of his cock and pressed it toward her opening. She turned her head and kissed the man behind her as the three engaged in an erotic tribal dance.

Not wanting to interrupt their concentration, my own hand fell to my crotch, and I began massaging my clit while I cupped and squeezed my breasts with my other hand. My mind raced ahead, thinking about all the different positions and permutations I could engage in with these three partners.

After a few minutes of erotic play, the man on the woman's backside angled his hips upward and the woman tilted her ass back to receive him. Their mouths opened in a silent moan as he slid his cock inside her. The man in front continued to hump the woman's belly, but now the woman had two hands free to clasp his cock and give him proper attention. As she and the man behind her rocked their hips together, the rainbow stripes slid over the other man's erection, making it look like a writhing anaconda.

How I wanted that cock inside me!

The movement of the man and the woman who were joined began to speed up and as I drooled from my soaking pussy, he slammed his hips against her ass, forcing her hands to move up and down on the other man's cock. She didn't need to do anything now, other than hold her hands tightly around his throbbing manhood. I was surprised how much of his organ I could see thrusting into the light, even with her grasping it hand-over-hand. It had to be at least nine inches long. As I inserted my fingers into my slit and began humping myself, I imagined directing it into my own quivering tunnel.

The three figures were now moving as one and their pace was accelerating toward an obvious climax. With one final thrust of his hips, the man in the rear slammed his cock deep inside the woman and pulled her hips toward his groin as he came inside her. I moaned out loud as my own climax rolled over me, our bodies heaving from the contractions consuming both of us. The man pulled his throbbing cock out of the woman's pussy and I could see it bobbing in the rainbow light as his seed coursed through his shaft. He leaned over and whispered something in the woman's ear, then left the room.

Now's as good a time as ever to make my entrance, I thought.

I figured I'd better get in there before the remaining couple got too hot and heavy. I wasn't sure if the man in front had come yet, but I sensed he wouldn't be disappointed to have *two* women in the enclosure giving him attention. I opened the door and stepped inside, and they turned toward me. The woman was still holding the man's dick in her hands, stroking it softly up and down. And he was still hard as a rock, in obvious need of satisfaction.

I walked up to the couple and without saying a word, I wrapped my hands around the woman's, feeling the heat emanating from the man's member. She released her hands to permit me freer access and I squeezed his pole tightly. It had to be at least six inches in circumference and even longer than I thought. I could feel him pulsating in my hands, and I leaned in to kiss him. He moaned softly as I flicked my thumb over his slick head, feeling his pre-cum leak onto my hand. The woman leaned forward and joined us in a three-way kiss while her hand cupped the man's balls.

I could feel his passion rising as the two of us gave him a glorious two-way handjob, but I wanted to save him for something else. There was no way I was going to let this beautiful cock go to waste by letting him cum in my hands. I began lowering myself, kissing his sculpted chest and washboard abs. His bush was neatly trimmed with just a bit of stubble on his pubis, and his balls were smooth as a baby's bottom. I really appreciated a man who shaved down there, especially one with such an impressive package.

When my head reached below his navel, I gobbled up the head of his tool like it was my last meal. I could only get about four inches of him inside my mouth, but I savored every bit of it with my swirling tongue. I hadn't sucked that many dicks in my life, but I knew a keeper when I saw one, and this was one spectacular johnson. While I sucked his manhood, the other woman moved behind him, squeezing his balls. Although maybe she was doing something *else* to him back there, because suddenly his hip movements escalated in urgency.

I didn't mind the idea of him cumming in my mouth, but I didn't want to siphon any of his virility before clamping another part of my body around his impressive python. I pulled my mouth off his cock and lifted myself up, licking his sweating torso with my open tongue. When I reached his face, I plunged my tongue into his mouth. The thrusting and swirling action left little doubt that I wanted to be properly fucked by him.

Screw the other girl, I thought. *She'd already gotten her piece of the action—now it was my turn.*

I turned around and began rubbing my slick ass against his dripping pole. Then I slipped his erection between my

cheeks and shifted slowly up and down, giving it a tanta-
lizing massage. He pulled back a little and grabbed his cock,
trying to steer it into my anus, but I wasn't having any of
that. Maybe later, if I was still in the mood, but right now I
needed that throbbing monster inside my pussy. I wanted to
feel him fucking me the old-fashioned way, filling me with
his manhood, stimulating my G-spot, stretching me to the
limit.

I reached between my legs and grabbed the sticky head
of his prick and directed it toward my wet opening. He was
only too happy to oblige, and after I poked it inside the front
door, he slowly pushed it in all the way. I gasped at the
thickness and depth of his intrusion as I clamped down on
his throbbing meat like a bear trap. There was no way I was
letting him escape until I was fully satisfied. He reached
around and grabbed my tits with both hands, squeezing
them gently while he thrust his shaft in and out of my love
canal. I could feel my clitoral hood sliding back and forth
over my nub as he pulled and stretched my labia with every
thrust of his giant cock.

I could have easily come from this movement without
any further stimulation, but as if reading my thoughts, the
woman circled around and began rubbing her breasts
against mine, heightening my ecstasy. As she kissed me
passionately, I began moaning and grunting from the pleasure consuming me. My hands wrapped around her waist as
I grasped her buttocks in each hand and pulled her toward
me with each thrust of the man behind. We both panted in
delight as we ground our pussies together.

Never had I felt such intense pleasure from so many
different sensations at the same time. This was my first
threesome, and it had already far exceeded my expectations.
I would have been happy to come this way, sandwiched

between two lovers, but perhaps sensing the newness of the experience for me, the woman pulled out of our lip lock and began to move her head down my body.

She cupped and played with my breasts, sucking and flicking my tender nipples with her soft, slippery tongue. I moaned, listening to the popping sound my erect nipples made when they slid in and out of her suckling mouth. I pulled her face into my chest, begging her to continue. But after a few minutes, she pulled away and moved lower. Slowly— tantalizingly—she kissed and nibbled her way down my body until she got to my soaking snatch. She paused and kissed it gently, then nibbled her way down the edges of my labia as the man slammed his cock in and out of me.

"Oh God!" I panted, practically fainting from the intensity of the pleasure building up inside me. The idea of being serviced on both ends by two different partners was driving me insane. I pushed my mound toward the woman's face and tilted my hips so my clit was level with her lips. When her tongue found my button and her lips surrounded me, I grabbed the back of her head with both hands and pulled her tightly toward me.

"Fuck, yes," I panted. "Fuck me," I shouted to no one in particular. I wanted to be fucked from both sides. *Fill me with your cock and flick me with your tongue,* I thought. *I want to soak you with my juices and feel you throbbing deep inside me.*

I slammed my mound into the woman's face and face-fucked her with all my energy as she sucked my clit into her mouth and rolled her tongue over its head. I was seconds away from having the strongest orgasm of my life.

"Yes—*yes!*" I screamed, as I bucked and whimpered from the intense pleasure racking my body. The man sensed I was about to come and I could feel his thrusting beginning to increase in intensity. I felt his hot breath on my back as he panted in unison with me. I looked down at the rainbow stripes washing over our thrashing bodies and closed my eyes, tilting my head back. This was as close to heaven as I could imagine.

When I was finally ready to come, I didn't hold anything back. I screamed like a wild animal, fucking the woman's face while the man slammed his python up inside me in a series of final rhythmic thrusts, spewing his honey inside me. I temporarily lost strength in my legs, but it didn't matter. The man's hard pole had me impaled like a cross, holding me suspended in the air as I gushed all over the woman's face.

When I finally stopped shaking and began to catch my breath, they both pulled away and turned to face me. We pressed together in a sublime three-way kiss, tasting each other's cum in our mouths. I opened my eyes and as I watched the spectrum of colors wash over our faces, and I couldn't help but smile.

I'd finally found my pot of gold at the end of the rainbow.

Mula Banha is for lovers...

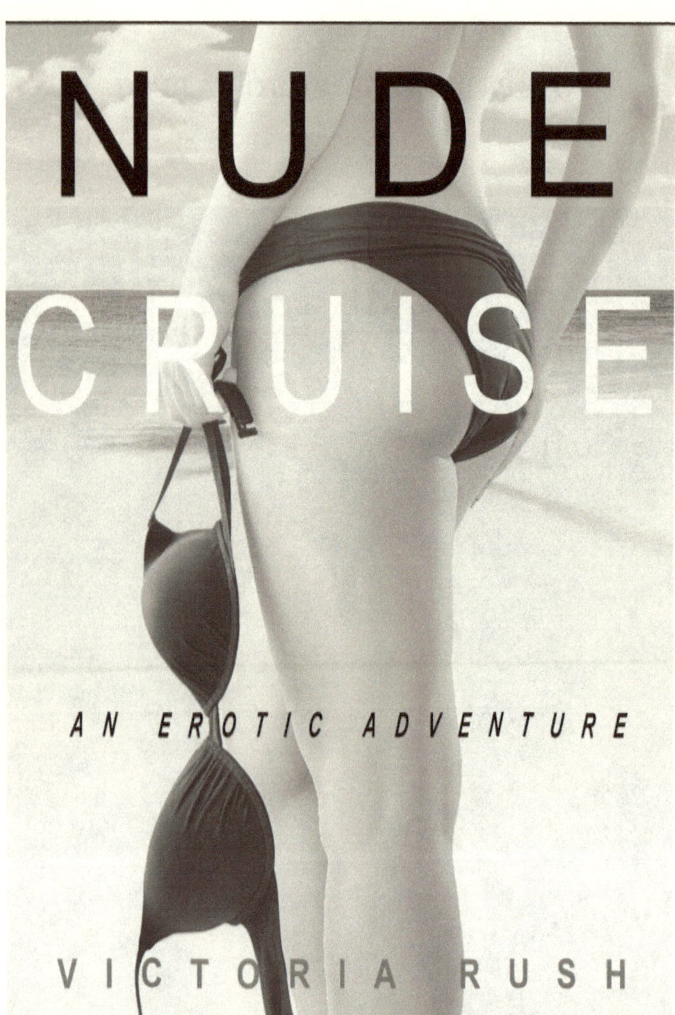

Some people get wet on a cruise for different reasons...

Some people can get into pretty tight spots on a crowded train...

Spying on the neighbors just got a lot more interesting...

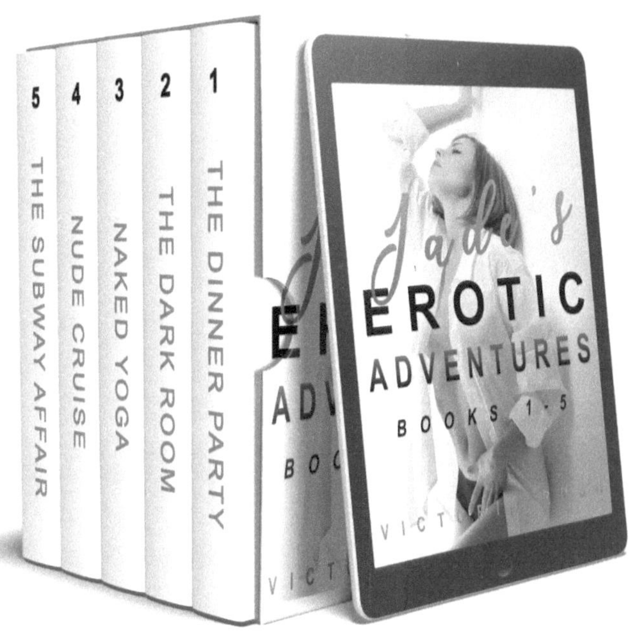

Enjoy the first five books in the bestselling series — now 60% off

NAKED YOGA - PREVIEW

MEDITATION

When I got to the naked yoga studio on my appointment day, I was pleasantly surprised. The room was bright, clean, and well-appointed, with tasteful prints on the wall, clean white sheers covering the windows, and a new hardwood floor. This wasn't some dingy pseudo-massage parlor operation as I'd feared.

I arrived ten minutes early, around the time other patrons were beginning to stream in. There was a mix of men and women in their twenties and thirties. Some of them appeared to be couples, judging by the intimacy of their hushed conversations and how close they huddled together. Before long, everybody staked out a spot on the floor and began stretching quietly on their mats.

At first, I was surprised to see everybody dressed in familiar yoga attire. But then I remembered what Soraya had said in our online chat conversation about everybody being asked to disrobe at the start of each session. I placed my purse and coat on a bench in a conspicuous place where I could keep an eye on it, then found an open spot on the floor and began stretching. I wasn't really interested in stretching yet, but it kept me busy and avoiding awkward glances with the people sitting around me.

During a transition in one of my stretches, I looked up and locked eyes with a pretty red-haired girl stretching beside me who couldn't have been much beyond her teens. She was wearing pink tights and a yellow top that pressed against her small but perky breasts. She didn't appear to be wearing a sports bra, and I could see the outline of her nipples as they pushed against soft cotton. We smiled at one another then returned to our stretching as we pretended to ignore the palpable tension in the room.

Shortly after, an attractive woman wearing matching Lululemon tops and bottoms walked toward the front of the room, where she placed a mat in front of the floor-to-ceiling mirrors lining the wall. She nodded and smiled at a few familiar faces, then looked at the large clock on the side wall. It was 7:00 p.m.

"Good evening, everyone," she said, addressing the room. "For those of you who are visiting us for the first time, welcome to our Tantric Yoga program, Level One — Meditations. For those of you who are returning, it's great to see you again. Remember that your progression through the levels should be at your leisure. You should step up to the next level only when you feel comfortable enough with the exercises and with your interaction with your fellow participants."

I wondered if she was Soraya from my chat session. My eyes ran up and down her body, analyzing ever contour of her perfectly shaped figure. Her legs were long and slim and bulging in all the right places. I marveled at the diamond shape of her calves and the line flexing up the side of her tights that separated her gently curved quadricep and hamstring muscles. Her Madonna-toned arms were slender and cut, and I could see the outline of her tricep muscles as she moved her arms. Her stomach was flat as a washboard, and her ample breasts swelled over the top of her tight-fitting top, above a tapering waist. She had a perfect athletic gymnast's figure, and I hoped she'd turn around for a moment to reveal an ass that I was sure I could bounce a coin off.

She was absolutely gorgeous, and I couldn't take my eyes off her. She had a vaguely European look, with dark brown hair, high cheekbones, and full rosebud lips. As I watched her talk, I imagined pressing my body against hers, kissing her in a passionate embrace. I couldn't wait for the program to start and see her gorgeous body in the buff.

As if reading my mind, she looked at me and smiled.

"My name's Alexandra," she said. "I'll be your instructor for today's session. Shall we get started?"

Everybody including me nodded.

"Our first order of business is to shed the trappings of modern civilization by dispensing with our clothes. These are just holding us back from truly connecting with our bodies and reaching our full potential. Yoga is intended to free our minds, bodies, and spirits. Practicing our craft in the nude will enable us to open our minds and experience true freedom and relaxation. Let's all disrobe now and place our garments on the floor beside your mats."

Alexandra reached over her shoulders and pulled her top over her head then bent over in a perfect pike position and pulled down her yoga pants. Then she nonchalantly stepped out of them and placed them in a neatly folded pile near the mirrors. I hesitated for a moment, soaking up her gorgeous body. Her B-cup tits stood proud and tall on her chiseled chest, with a thin indentation running down the front of her abdomen to her perfectly bald pubis.

When she turned around and bent over to place her clothes on the floor, I gasped out loud. Her ass was as tight and round as a schoolgirl's. The muscles in her glutes flexed as she stretched and contracted them from the bending motion. When she turned back around, I suddenly became aware that I was the only person in the room who was still clothed. I awkwardly pulled my tights off with everybody watching me, then placed them on the floor beside my mat. I could see myself reflected in the mirrors at the front of the room and part of me wanted to move my hands in front of my pussy to cover up. But everyone else seemed perfectly relaxed being naked, and I scanned the expanse of mirrors to take in the sight.

There were about fifteen people in the room, in various shapes and colors. Some had dark bodies, and some had fair skin like me. Most were slim and toned, but there were a few curvy girls with full breasts and wide hips. I noticed two men standing near the back of the pack, and I wondered if they'd chosen this position out of shyness or because it offered the best position for viewing the women's bare backsides. I squinted to see if I could detect any sign of tumescence in their hanging members, but they appeared to be fully relaxed and flaccid. I was glad that they'd also trimmed their bushes short and neat so as not to interfere with maximum viewing pleasure.

"Right, then," Alexandra said. "Now that we're fully free to relax and connect with our bodies, I'd like everyone to lie down on your mats face up and place your arms gently at your side. Close your eyes and breathe in slowly through your nostrils, then exhale deeply to remove the troubles of your day. Try to empty your mind and focus on the beauty and serenity of your body."

It was strange lying on my yoga mat completely naked, knowing I was surrounded by so many people in a similar state of undress. I was tempted to turn my head and open my eyes to steal another glance at Alexandra or the girl beside me, but I followed her instructions and focused on my breathing. It felt liberating to take my clothes off around like-minded strangers, and I could feel myself begin to relax as a cool draft swept over my body. The stillness in the room was a welcome respite from my hectic workday.

After two or three minutes, Alexandra instructed us to open our eyes and sit up on our mats in the Buddha position.

"Cross your legs, bringing your heels under your knees, then lift your chest so your spine is straight. You may open your eyes if you wish, as you can begin to feel comfortable in your natural body among your peers."

I raised my eyelids and turned my head slowly to look around the room. The young girl beside me caught my gaze and looked straight into my eyes. I smiled at her as her eyes drifted down my chest and she looked at my exposed breasts and stomach. I unconsciously lifted my chest and pushed my tits out as far as I could. My breasts were much larger than hers, and I was proud of how firm and high they still stood at my age. I could feel my nipples hardening and I blushed slightly as I glanced at her tight figure.

Her skin was flawlessly smooth and unblemished, and she had barely an ounce of fat anywhere on her body. Her small boobs seemed to be glued onto her chest, as if somebody had sculpted them out of clay. They barely moved as she breathed in and out, rising in tandem with her expanding ribs and diaphragm. Her nipples were small, with pinched areolas betraying her excitement. Maybe it was just the cool air circulating in the room, but her nipples were definitely standing out in an aroused state. I lifted my eyes and we smiled at each other, in tacit approval of each other's physiques.

I frowned when Alexandra interrupted our connection, instructing us to change position.

"Now that we're getting comfortable in our natural bodies," she said, "let's expand our horizons and begin to stretch our capabilities. I'd like you to extend your legs straight in front of you and gently flex your toes toward your knees. Now, gently lean forward with a straight spine and run your hands along the top of your tights toward your feet until you feel some gentle pressure in your hamstrings. Hold the position, breathing slowly and deeply, until you feel your muscles relax, then push forward another inch, trying to move your head as close to your knees as possible."

My flexibility was pretty good from my regular yoga classes, so I was able to get all the way down and I rest my chest on my thighs, clasping my hands around the undersides of my feet. I looked in Alexandra's direction and she nodded approvingly while holding a similar position without any sign of strain in her face. I turned my head and peeked under my outstretched arm at the young girl beside me and she did the same. We both giggled for a moment, then placed our heads back between our knees and concentrated on our poses. I could feel the mat underneath me beginning to moisten between my legs as I began to think about what I'd like to do with her at the next level in our training.

After another three or four minutes, Alexandra instructed us to move into the next position.

"You're all doing wonderfully," she said. "Now we're going

to move into a new position to really give those hammies a workout. Bring the sole of your right foot to rest against your left inner thigh. Now, turn and extend your chest over your left knee, holding your left leg or foot to gently pull yourself forward. As before, breathe slowly and hold the position when it begins to bind, then extend yourself forward in small increments as you feel the pressure in your hamstring slowly relax. Go as far as you can without feeling uncomfortable. Your goal is to elongate your muscles and improve your flexibility so you can be ready for whatever tight spots life throws at us in the real world."

I was feeling a tight spot between my legs, and I pressed the heel of my right foot hard against my pussy. This was the first time I'd actively touched myself in the session, and I began to think about what might be in store as I moved to the more advanced classes and begin to interact more closely with other participants. I hoped that the girl to my side with whom I'd made a silent connection would be there so we could partner up and explore our bodies more intimately.

Alexandra instructed us to switch sides and extend our right leg to stretch the opposite hamstring. The girl and I glanced quickly again at each other before we bent down, and I began to fantasize about going down on her. I wiggled my hips against my left heel, trying to increase the friction against my swollen clit. But Alexandra always seemed to interrupt our poses before I could work up enough sustained contact to go very far.

Perhaps this was by design, to create just enough contact with ourselves and others to make us yearn for a stronger connection with our partners. I had to admire the brilliance of their business model. They were building a powerful desire to move on to the next stage. Just as with normal sex, no one in their right mind wanted to stop before achieving the pinnacle of pleasure.

"Okay," Alexandra said, interrupting my thoughts once again. "Now we're going to try a variation on this pose that will help us stretch our ribcages and build our core. Bring your right forearm down to the inside of your right leg and try to grab the inside of your right foot. Then reach up and over your head with your other arm. Rotate your left palm inward and try to clasp the outer edge of your right foot while rotating your chest inwards and upwards."

A few people near the back of the room grunted and groaned as they tried the awkward maneuver.

"I know," Alexandra said, "this is a tough one. Just go as far as you feel comfortable without feeling undue strain. As always, pause at the moment of tension and breathe deeply. Feel your tummy pushing in and out as you use your diaphragm to breathe from your belly, not your chest. Glance up toward the ceiling to encourage your body to twist as much as you can. When you begin to relax, push a little further and hold."

This time, the girl next to me and I were facing each other directly, only a few feet apart. We looked at each other and giggled again. We were definitely forming a connection as we ran each other's eyes shamelessly down and across each other's bodies, watching the muscles in our stomachs rippling from the tension of the side stretch. We both had our heels in front of our bare crotches, which only added to the titillation of the pose. I tried to will her to pull her foot away to give me a glimpse of her naked pussy, but we remained obedient to Alexandra's instruction.

Just as I was beginning to think the sequence of poses had been carefully staged to reveal only enough of our bodies to our fellow participants to build an unquenchable desire, Alexandra instructed us to sit up and change position once again.

"Now let's focus on another important element of our core strength, which is our lower back. Sit up and place your legs directly in front of you once again, then bend your right leg until your right heel is touching the inside of your left knee. Now reach up with your left arm and twist toward your right side with your right hand on the floor beside you, placing your left elbow on the outside of your elevated knee. You should feel a gentle stretch in your lower back and glutes. Look behind you and find a spot on the wall where you can focus, then gently try to twist your body further in that direction as you trace a line further along the wall toward your right. Hold, breathe, and relax. Then twist a little further, pushing yourself to twist as far as you feel comfortable."

My gaze was averted away from the girl next to me, so I scanned the room behind me. I could see the two men at the back of the room stretching in the seated twist position, looking just as serious and focused as the rest of us. I caught a few people stealing furtive glances at one another, but for the most part everybody seemed lost in the moment concentrating on their poses, seemingly mindless of their naked and exposed positions.

Alexandra asked us to switch and turn to the other side, which gave me an opportunity to scan the other side of the room. I noticed some of the women glancing in my direction and we smiled as we checked out each other's bodies. So far, the experience had been liberating and mildly stimulating, but I was beginning to grow tired with how we'd been covering up our most erogenous parts with the poses Alexandra had led us through.

"Okay," she said, as if reading my mind. "Now we're going

to get a little more risqué in our positions and open up our bodies to channel our chi more freely."

She sat up on her mat and extended her legs straight in front of her. Then she slowly spread her legs apart, exposing her bare vulva to the entire room. My breathing quickened and I became mindful of the growing wet spot on my mat. The slit in her pussy beckoned to me as I unconsciously leaned forward.

"We're going to do a wide-angle seated forward bend, which will stretch and strengthen your adductors and pubococcygeus muscle. I want you to spread your legs straight out and as far to the sides in front of you, then lean forward with a straight back as you reach out with your hands toward your outstretched feet. You'll feel a tightness between your legs, so you have to do this slowly and carefully so as not to pull anything."

Alexandra leaned forward and clasped her heels with her two hands and pulled herself forward until her chest rested on the floor. There was no denying that she was extremely flexible, as she moved through each of the poses to the maximum extent possible with little noticeable strain.

As I mimicked her movement, I tried not to glance between the legs of the yoga partners in front of me. I wished the young girl who'd I'd made a connection with had been positioned in front of me instead of to my side. As I leaned forward, I turned my head and glanced in her direction. She did the same, and we moved our chests forward and down in a synchronized manner. If yoga was all about the union of mind and body, I definitely was feeling yoked with my fantasy yoga partner.

"Press your pelvis into the floor," Alexandra said. "Bring your chest down and forward as far as you can. Spread your thighs apart with your hands as you feel the tension between your legs relax."

I glanced around the room and watched all the toned men and women bending over spreading their legs. My pussy grew wetter and wetter until I could hear the squishing of my legs against the mat as I rubbed my clit back and forth in the small puddle beneath me. I glanced over at the girl next to me and she smiled knowingly, as my pace of breathing increased and my eyes began to glaze over. I could have sworn her hips were rocking back and forth in lockstep with mine as we fantasized about rubbing our pussies together.

Please, I pleaded with her under my breath. *Please come back to the next session.*

Just when I was getting close to having a mini-orgasm, Alexandra asked us to sit up and change position.

Damn, girl, I thought. *You're such a tease.*

I was more convinced than ever that these poses were orchestrated to maximize the arc of our arousal just enough to deny us ultimate pleasure, so we'd have no choice but to come back and finish the deal.

"You're all doing fabulous," she purred in her soft, gentle intonation. "Now I want you to sit up with a straight back with your legs still spread out in front of you."

My eyes widened as she grabbed her big toes and began to lift them off the floor until they were at the same height as her head. She had opened herself up completely to the room, exposing her bare pussy and breasts in the most revealing way, daring us to ravish her magnificent body with our eyes.

"This is one of our most liberating poses," she said as she held her feet in the air, "where you'll feel most at one with your bodies and with those of your fellow yogis."

She glanced toward the back of the room at the two men and looked down between their legs.

"Don't worry if you notice some of your partners in a state of obvious arousal. This is a normal and healthy response and is just another way for us to connect with our bodies and feel the energy flowing through us. Try to keep your back straight and look up toward the ceiling as you lift your chest and breathe deeply. Feel your connection to the universe and the power within your own bodies. Free your mind and let all the negative chi flow from your body."

As I spread my legs and prepared to move into the provocative position, I rotated my hips slightly so I'd be facing closer to the girl next to me. I didn't want to make it too obvious what I was doing, but I was hoping she'd do the same so that we could look at one another's fully exposed bodies and I could let my fantasies run free. I began to lift my legs at a forty-five-degree angle to her and noticed out the corner of my eye that she had shifted her body subtly toward mine in a similar manner.

"Try to flex your PC muscle as you feel your Mula Bandha tighten and relax," Alexandra said. "This will create a stronger connection during intimate moments with your partner and heighten your sexual pleasure."

As I extended my legs and revealed my glistening pussy for the entire room to see, I looked over at the girl and smiled triumphantly. We'd opened ourselves up to one another in every sense of the word and let all of our inhibitions fall away while reveling in the beauty of one another's bodies. She was still turned just far enough away that I couldn't see her bare pussy behind her outstretched leg, but I noticed the puddle on the mat just in front of her.

She was just as turned on as I was!

My pussy quivered and shook in the excitement of the

moment. If anyone had touched me anywhere near my Mula Bandha, I would have had an orgasm in a millisecond. My mind raced with all the possibilities I could engage in with my fantasy partner during the next level session. Just when I thought it couldn't get any more intense and intimate at that moment, Alexandra gave us a new instruction.

"Now," she said, "while still holding your toes as high in the air as you can, gently lean back with a straight back until you're balancing on your buttocks in a spread piked position."

She demonstrated the technique as she tipped slowly backwards then held a perfect forty-five degree piked position, looking up toward the ceiling in the sexiest but most composed manner.

God, I thought. *I'd fuck that woman any day—in any position.*

I glanced over at the girl behind me, and we both leaned backwards at the same time, matching the degree of rotation in perfect synchronicity. When we both reached the same forty-five-degree angle of our backs towards the floor, we beamed at one another in joy and pride at having achieved this level of proficiency. I wanted to turn my body completely in her direction and scoot my ass over to her then wrap my legs around her while we ground our pussies together and kissed passionately.

This naked yoga thing was even hotter than I'd hoped! I knew I'd be counting the minutes until the next session in horny anticipation.

I glanced in the mirror to see how this was working for the two men and saw that they had full hard-ons, angled straight up at forty-five degrees in the same direction as their outspread legs. What a turn-on this must have been for everybody in the room!

"I'm very proud of all of you," Alexandra said, as she began to lower her legs back toward the mat. "Now it's time for us to relax and return to a quiet state. Please bring your legs back onto your mats and cross them in front of you in the seated Buddha position. Close your eyes and reflect back on the growth you've achieved today. Breathe slowly in and out and feel the energy coursing through your body. You've all come a long way today. If you feel comfortable moving on to the next level, I hope to see you again where we'll explore a new level of synergy working together to stretch our minds and spirits even further."

Alexandra closed her eyes and placed the back of her hands on her knees as she touched her thumbs and forefingers together.

"Om," she chanted, exhaling slowly in an extended intonation.

"Om..." the room chanted with her in harmony, as our spirits exalted.

There was no question that I was ready to take this to the next level. I glanced out the corner of my eye at the girl next to me and winked as she returned my gaze.

I hope we'll see each other in a whole new light the next time we meet, I smiled to myself.

Read More

ABOUT THE AUTHOR

If you would like to receive notification of new book(s) in Jade's Erotic Adventures, follow me at http://bookbub.com/authors/victoria-rush.

If you have a moment, please post a brief review on my Amazon book page at viewbook.at/dr . Even just a couple of sentences will help other readers find and enjoy this book as much as you hopefully did.

Follow, share, like, and comment at:

www.facebook.com/authorvictoriarush
www.pinterest.com/authorvictoriarush
www.twitter.com/authorvictoriarush
authorvictoriarush@outlook.com

Hope to see you again soon!

www.ingramcontent.com/pod-product-compliance
Lightning Source LLC
Chambersburg PA
CBHW021206110726

47900CB00002B/748